To Arlene, my beautiful and intelligent wife and our six children—Andrew, Lucy, Douglas, Louise, David, and Samuel: "Wherever you are the light shines."

Thank you Missy Sisson for your excellent assistance. Thank you Andrew for your persistance in encouraging me to write *The Parrot Man* after I regularly told it to the children at bedtime over many years.

Thank you Yasushi, for bringing the Parrot Man to life through your great illustrations. And lest we forget, thank you Daniel for your superb editorial assistance.

www.mascotbooks.com

The Parrot Man: A Baseball Story

For more information, please contact:
Mascot Books
620 Herndon Parkway, Suite 320
Herndon, VA 20170
info@mascotbooks.com

Library of Congress Control Number: 2017915635

CPSIA Code: PRT0418A
ISBN-13: 978-1-68401-212-1

Printed in the United States

THE PARROT MAN

A BASEBALL STORY

Written by
MACKNIGHT BLACK

Epilogue by
David S. Black

Illustrated by
YASUSHI MATSUOKA

LITTLE BARNEY differed from the other children in his Baltimore orphanage. He had deep-set gray eyes beneath a heavy brow, a large head, short neck, and a barreled chest tapering to narrow hips and spindly legs. His voice often produced a loud, grating sound.

When people came to the orphanage to select a child, the children rushed into the visitors' room. Little Barney would position himself at the front of the herd and run around the room hollering. No one ever chose him.

By the time he turned ten, Barney realized adoption would not happen for him. He stopped showing up in the visitors' room and became reclusive. What kept him going was a staff worker who told him his father had been a great baseball player. More than anything, Barney wanted to play major league baseball. In time, however, his small size and lack of coordination worked against him. He often stayed in his room and listened to the Washington Senators' games on the radio.

ONE DAY while Barney listened to a game, the staff worker walked by his room. "What are you doing inside on such a beautiful day with the other boys playing outside?" she asked. "Come with me."

Outside, the staff worker told the boys playing baseball to include Barney. The captain put Barney in right field. "This is an important game," he said. "Don't mess up."

Barney's team led 2-1 in the ninth inning. With the other team's runners on second and third base, a fly ball found Barney in the outfield. He raised his glove to make the catch but flubbed it. Both base runners scored. Barney's team lost, 3-2. His teammates went berserk. "You stink, stupid Barney. We lost the championship because of you."

After that, Barney did not play baseball, though he still read about major league teams and listened to games on the radio.

AT EIGHTEEN, Barney left the orphanage. He moved to Washington, D.C., where his caring staff worker found him a job selling newspapers outside of Griffith Stadium where the Washington Senators of that era played.

One August day after Barney sold all his papers, he bought a ticket and entered the stadium. He sat in the left field bleachers.

In a middle inning, the Senators had the bases loaded. A fly ball floated toward the Detroit Tigers' left fielder playing directly below where Barney sat. Barney emitted a frightening cry conveying despair, anger, and hope. The confused left fielder turned toward the noise from the bleachers and missed the ball. All three of the Senators' base runners scored.

"WHAT WAS THAT?" asked a fan.

"It was that little fella over there."

"We need more yells like that to motivate these bums."

In the next inning, Detroit's best hitter stood in the batter's box. A fan turned to Barney: "Give us another yell, man." Barney unleashed his haunting cries as the pitcher pitched, the batter froze, and the umpire called, "Strike three!"

"Parrot Man, where have you been?" a fan asked. "We need you." At that moment, the Parrot Man was born. For the rest of the game, and for many seasons after that, he yelled and yelled such unique shouts as "cut-h-oo," "wootsie-bootsie-hi," "caw-caw-caw," and "w-a-hoo-wi, w-a-hoo-wi!"

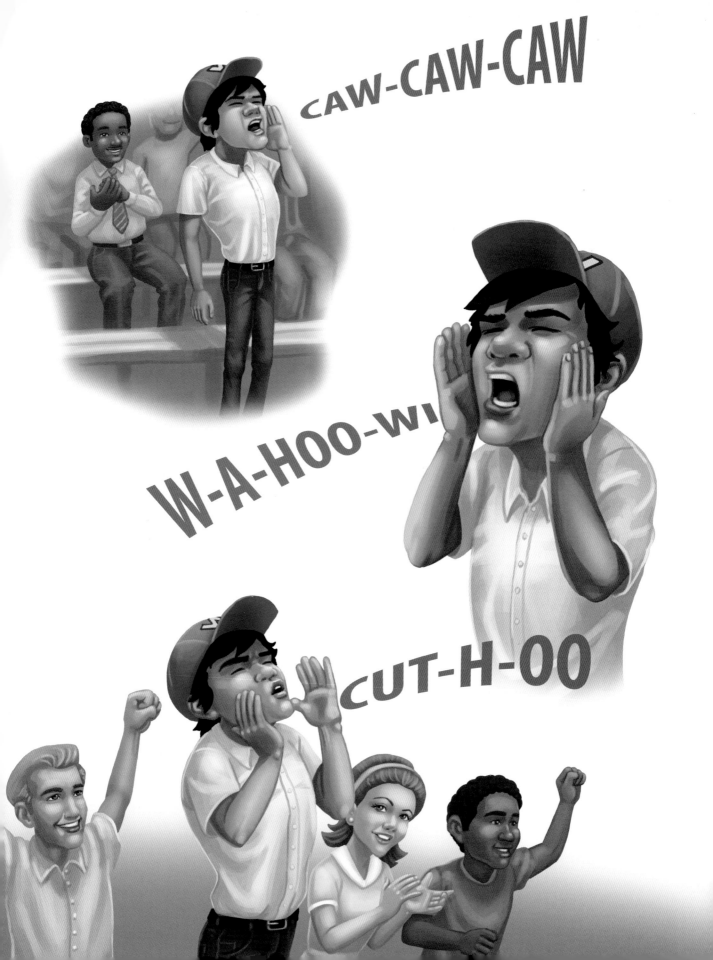

EVENTUALLY, the Parrot Man saved enough money to attend about half of the Senators' home games each season. He became a fixture at the ballpark, shouting more and more. His voice echoed throughout the stadium.

After a while, however, as the poor play of the Senators continued and the novelty of the Parrot Man wore off, the fans' attitude toward him changed.

"Hey fella, give us a break. Quiet down."

"Freak, don't you ever shut up?"

"Stay home sometimes so we can enjoy the game!"

NOT DISCOURAGED, the Parrot Man started bringing his baseball glove to the games and began his quest to catch a baseball hit into the stands. He put all of his savings into a season ticket. He chose a seat in the upper deck between home plate and first base, where he believed most foul balls landed. He had his glove at every game but didn't catch a ball.

As the years passed, the Parrot Man became increasingly obsessed and frustrated. He would jump to his feet as soon as a foul ball headed in his direction. He ran with his glove-hand outstretched, jumping across seats, and banging into fans. He knocked down one fan and bruised others during his mad dashes.

People began complaining to the Senators' management. They signed a petition asking that he be expelled from the ballpark.

12

ONE EVENING before the game began, a Senators' official asked him to come to his office where he said: "Stop chasing after foul balls, or we will have to revoke your season ticket and order you to stay out of Griffith Stadium."

WITHOUT COMMENT, the Parrot Man dejectedly left the office and returned to his seat where a boy and a man sat down in front of him. "It's so great being at my first big league game with you, Pa," said the boy. "I thought this night would never get here. I've missed you so much."

"I miss you too, Andy—more than I can say," said the man. "But there are circumstances I can't control—like your mother and me divorced and my job located in Boston with you a Washingtonian. But we didn't come here to be sad. We go to baseball games to have fun and forget our troubles."

"You're right, Pa. That's easy to do out here."

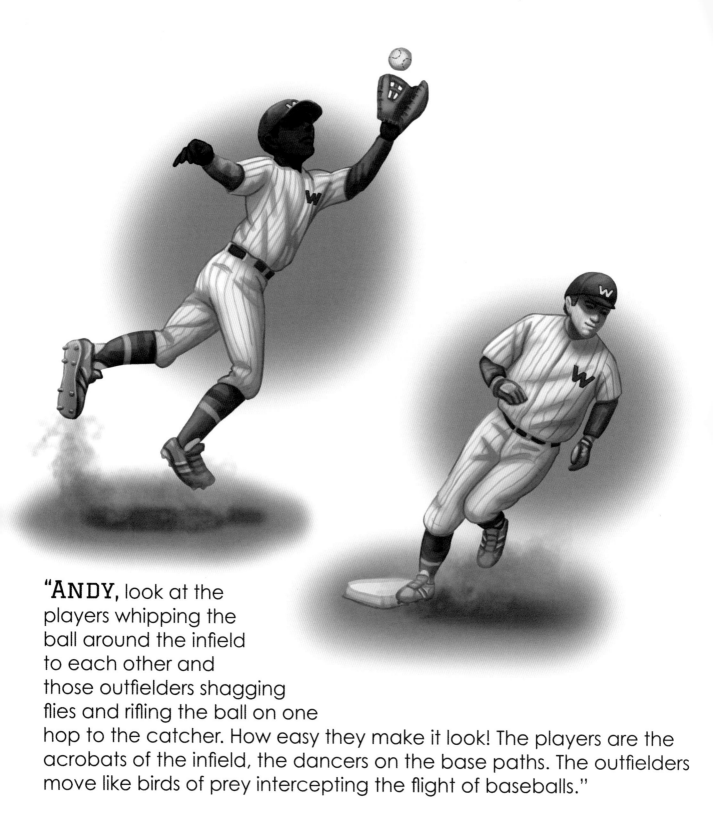

"ANDY, look at the
players whipping the
ball around the infield
to each other and
those outfielders shagging
flies and rifling the ball on one
hop to the catcher. How easy they make it look! The players are the
acrobats of the infield, the dancers on the base paths. The outfielders
move like birds of prey intercepting the flight of baseballs."

"That's what I want to do, Pa. Play major league baseball when I
grow up."

16

"JUST REMEMBER, ANDY, you have to be so good to play in the big leagues. Of the millions of kids playing baseball and dreaming of becoming big leaguers, these are the few who make it, the handful of truly great athletes who beat all the competition in running, hitting, throwing, catching, and having instant, correct reactions to what's happening in the game."

THE PARROT MAN leaned forward with great interest. A tear rolled down his cheek and splashed silently on the concrete at his feet. He did not bother to wipe his eyes, so intently did he listen as the man and the boy talked inning after inning of their love of baseball and their joy at attending the game together.

"Look at how beautiful it is out there," the man said. "How all those lights shining down from their towers intensify the scene—the freshly cut greenest grass and the white chalked foul lines on their eternal journeys to the foul poles. Smell the cigar smoke, popcorn, peanuts, beer, hot dogs, onions, mustard, and ketchup. The divine aromas of baseball!"

"You know, Pa," the boy said, "I feel so super-terrific being with you at this game. I feel like I could just reach up and grab one of those old stars right out of the night." He pointed toward the black, star sprinkled sky beyond the lights of the ball park.

THE PARROT MAN looked up in the direction the boy pointed. A mighty white light descended toward him like a falling star streaming diamond-like sparkles behind it. Down, down, down came the object. The Parrot Man stepped out into the aisle, raised his gloved hand and calmly, gracefully caught the baseball.

HE STARED at the ball for a moment. He held it against his cheek, pressed it to his lips, turned it over and over in his glove examining its magnificence.

Several thousands were there that night to see the New York Yankees play the Washington Senators. No one said a word. Then a nearby fan exclaimed, "Hey! It's the Parrot Man! He finally caught one!"

A woman shouted, "IT IS THE PARROT MAN! BLESS HIS HEART! THE PARROT MAN GOT HIS BALL!"

The word rippled throughout the stadium. The crowd began to clap and cheer, but the Parrot Man ignored the ovation. Instead, he saw the boy standing beside him, gazing rapturously at the baseball. The Parrot Man hurriedly stuffed the baseball into his pocket, turned— and then he hesitated. The direct gaze of the boy met his eyes.

Slowly, he withdrew the ball from his pocket and placed it in the upturned palm of the boy's hand. He cupped the boy's other hand over the top of the baseball and whispered into the boy's ear, "Don't drop it, son." Then he turned and walked up the aisle, shoulders back, head held high until he disappeared from sight.

THE FRONT PAGE of the next day's *Washington Post* contained a picture of the Parrot Man handing the baseball to the spellbound boy. The caption beneath the picture read: "Barney Ross of our town, for many years a salesman for this newspaper and an ardent supporter of the Washington Senators, gives a baseball he just caught last night at Griffith Stadium to an unidentified boy. The Yankees beat the Senators 11-1."

The Parrot Man was seen no more at the ballpark. People phoned the Senators' management and wrote letters to *The Washington Post* asking what had happened to him. But he never returned. The only trace of the Parrot Man was his battered old outfielder's glove lying at the curb on Georgia Avenue outside of Griffith Stadium.

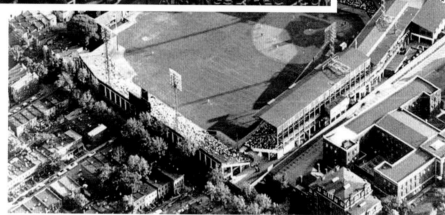

Griffith Stadium
Photo © National
Baseball Hall
of Fame and
Museum,
Cooperstown, NY

EPILOGUE

Griffith Stadium

by David Scott Black

GRIFFITH STADIUM, the site of much of the action in *The Parrot Man*, is worthy of a story by itself. This quirky, slapdash facility enjoyed a rich 50-year history filled with Presidents tossing ceremonial pitches, tape measure home runs by baseball icons such as Mickey Mantle, Josh Gibson, and Harmon Killebrew, jaw dropping pitching wizardry by Walter Johnson, and two gatherings of baseball's All-Stars. It was also the location of a single shining moment of baseball glory in 1924 and an extended period of baseball futility and failure during its last 28 years.

Griffith Stadium was located on a plot of land in Washington, D.C., bounded by Georgia Avenue to the west, W Street to the north, 5th Street to the east, and U Street to the south. An earlier wooden structure had housed professional baseball at the site since at least 1891. Although Griffith Stadium was a contemporary of the great steel and concrete parks constructed during the 1910s (such as Wrigley Field, Tiger Stadium, Ebbets Field, and Fenway Park), its hasty origins and some stubborn neighbors made it more peculiar than its classic brethren. The stadium's first iteration was constructed in just three weeks in 1911 when the prior wooden structure burned to the ground only a month before opening day. Work on the new park continued during Senators' road trips, and the stadium was completed on July 24, 1911. It was initially called National

Park, but this was changed to Griffith Stadium in 1923 when the structure was expanded and became the namesake of Clark Griffith, the Senators' manager from 1912-20 and owner from 1920-55. The stadium remained largely unaltered after 1923, except for the addition of lights and the introduction of night baseball on May 28, 1941.

Although the initial seating capacity was cozy (just 27,410), the playing dimensions were cavernous. The left field line stretched 407 feet from home plate. The right field wall was 31 feet high (just six feet shorter than Fenway Park's "Green Monster"). Right-center field was actually a longer distance from home plate (457 feet) than center field (421 feet) because the outfield fence jutted sharply and awkwardly into the playing field to accommodate five row houses and an oak tree that the Senators' ownership was unable to purchase from neighboring holdout property owners. The extreme dimensions made Griffith Stadium hostile to home runs but a haven for triples.

Griffith Stadium was the site of much memorable baseball history and one notable tradition that survives to this day. The World Series was played at Griffith Stadium in 1924, 1925, and 1933. It was the site of the All-Star Game in 1937 and 1956. During the 1940s, Hall of Fame slugger Josh Gibson and the mighty Homestead Grays of the Negro Leagues played there. In 1953, Mickey Mantle reportedly hit a 565-foot home run that exited Griffith Stadium after flying over the left field bleachers. The greatest Senator to make Griffith Stadium his home field was the incomparable Walter Johnson. Despite a team that lost far more games than it won during his 20-year career, the "Big Train" sported a 411-279 record with an incredible 110 shutouts and 3,508 strikeouts.

Griffith Stadium was also the birthplace of one of baseball's most enduring rituals: the ceremonial first pitch tossed by the President of the United States on Opening Day. Starting with William Howard Taft in 1910 and continuing through John F. Kennedy in 1961, nine different Presidents threw out the season's first pitch at Griffith Stadium a total of 37 times. The Senators even built a special Presidential Box next to the first base dugout just for the occasion.

The high point of baseball achievement at Griffith Stadium occurred on October 10, 1924, when the Senators defeated the New York Giants in the bottom of the twelfth inning of the deciding seventh game of the World Series. Senators' centerfielder Earl McNeely hit a routine ground ball that took a miraculous high hop over the head of Giants' third baseman Freddie Lindstrom to drive in catcher Muddy Ruel from second base, bringing Washington its first, and to this day, only World Series championship. *Washington Post* sportswriter Shirley Povich described the aftermath: "In Griffith Stadium the crowd catapulted out of the stands to thrash onto the field and to dance on the dugout roofs, refusing to leave the park until long after nightfall."

But baseball glory did not last long at Griffith Stadium. After the Senators' last World Series appearance in 1933 (this time, a 4-1 series loss to the Giants), Washington endured nearly three decades of baseball futility. During the 28 seasons from 1934 through 1961 (the last year baseball was played in Griffith Stadium), the Senators posted a winning record just four times and finished higher than fourth in the American League only three times. During this time, the Senators never finished first or appeared in the postseason. Washington was known as the city that was "first in war, first in peace, and last in the American League." Despite the long stretch of mediocrity on the field, Washington baseball fans, like the Parrot Man, grew to love and find comfort in the rituals, traditions, and happy distractions of baseball. With hopeless teams year after year, Washingtonians were drawn to Griffith Stadium by the game itself.

After five decades of providing a home to professional baseball in Washington, Griffith Stadium became a victim of progress and modernity. In 1962, the Senators moved to the newly opened D.C. Stadium (later renamed RFK Stadium), a multi-purpose facility with a perfectly arching centerfield wall and rationally symmetrical playing field. The last baseball game at Griffith Stadium was played on September 21, 1961 – a 6-3 loss to the Minnesota Twins.

After sitting vacant, Griffith Stadium was demolished in 1965. Howard University Hospital was constructed in its place and still stands to this day. Inside the hospital, in a hallway near a bank of elevators, is a marker showing the location of home plate at the old stadium, a reminder of a place where men played a boys' game, and boys at the park dreamed of catching that elusive foul ball.

Other Sources

History of Griffith Stadium

http://www.ballparksofbaseball.com/ballparks/griffith-stadium/

https://en.wikipedia.org/wiki/Griffith_Stadium

http://www.thisgreatgame.com/ballparks-griffith-stadium.html

https://en.wikipedia.org/wiki/Boundary_Field

Map Showing Location of Griffith Stadium: http://cdn.ghostsofdc.org/wp-content/uploads/2014/01/27131254/ca000102.jpg

Presidential First Pitch: https://en.wikipedia.org/wiki/Ceremonial_first_pitch

Washington Senators Year-by-Year Record: https://www.baseball-reference.com/teams/MIN/index.shtml

Howard University Hospital Home Plate Marker: https://www.deadballbaseball.com/?tag=howard-university-hospital

Walter Johnson: https://en.wikipedia.org/wiki/Walter_Johnson

Homestead Grays: https://en.wikipedia.org/wiki/Homestead_Grays

MACKNIGHT BLACK

Macknight attended the Episcopal Academy in suburban Philadelphia and graduated high school from Kent School in Kent, Connecticut. At Princeton he received an AB Degree in English.

He has served as a peace officer for the Children's Society in New York City; a book publisher's representative including manuscript scouting and book sales at colleges and universities (including Harvard and MIT) for the McGraw-Hill Book Co.; and the first administrative officer for the U.S. Department of Education's Title 1 Program that supports the education of economically deprived and educationally disadvantaged children.